Samuel French Acting Edition

Romance Novels for Dummies

by Boo Killebrew

D1525602

SAMUEL FRENCH

SAMUELFRENCH.COM SAMUELFRENCH.CO.UK

Copyright © 2017 by Boo Killebrew
All Rights Reserved

ROMANCE NOVELS FOR DUMMIES is fully protected under the copyright laws of the United States of America, the British Commonwealth, including Canada, and all other countries of the Copyright Union. All rights, including professional and amateur stage productions, recitation, lecturing, public reading, motion picture, radio broadcasting, television and the rights of translation into foreign languages are strictly reserved.

ISBN 978-0-573-70584-7

www.SamuelFrench.com
www.SamuelFrench.co.uk

FOR PRODUCTION ENQUIRIES

UNITED STATES AND CANADA
Info@SamuelFrench.com
1-866-598-8449

UNITED KINGDOM AND EUROPE
Plays@SamuelFrench.co.uk
020-7255-4302

Each title is subject to availability from Samuel French, depending upon country of performance. Please be aware that *ROMANCE NOVELS FOR DUMMIES* may not be licensed by Samuel French in your territory. Professional and amateur producers should contact the nearest Samuel French office or licensing partner to verify availability.

CAUTION: Professional and amateur producers are hereby warned that *ROMANCE NOVELS FOR DUMMIES* is subject to a licensing fee. Publication of this play(s) does not imply availability for performance. Both amateurs and professionals considering a production are strongly advised to apply to Samuel French before starting rehearsals, advertising, or booking a theatre. A licensing fee must be paid whether the title(s) is presented for charity or gain and whether or not admission is charged. Professional/Stock licensing fees are quoted upon application to Samuel French.

No one shall make any changes in this title(s) for the purpose of production. No part of this book may be reproduced, stored in a retrieval system, or transmitted in any form, by any means, now known or yet to be invented, including mechanical, electronic, photocopying, recording, videotaping, or otherwise, without the prior written permission of the publisher. No one shall upload this title(s), or part of this title(s), to any social media websites.

For all enquiries regarding motion picture, television, and other media rights, please contact Samuel French.

MUSIC USE NOTE

Licensees are solely responsible for obtaining formal written permission from copyright owners to use copyrighted music in the performance of this play and are strongly cautioned to do so. If no such permission is obtained by the licensee, then the licensee must use only original music that the licensee owns and controls. Licensees are solely responsible and liable for all music clearances and shall indemnify the copyright owners of the play(s) and their licensing agent, Samuel French, against any costs, expenses, losses and liabilities arising from the use of music by licensees. Please contact the appropriate music licensing authority in your territory for the rights to any incidental music.

IMPORTANT BILLING AND CREDIT REQUIREMENTS

If you have obtained performance rights to this title, please refer to your licensing agreement for important billing and credit requirements.

ROMANCE NOVELS FOR DUMMIES premiered at the Williamstown Theatre Festival in Williamston, Massachusetts in July 2016 under the direction of Moritz von Stuelpnagel, with sets by Timothy Mackabee, costumes by Tilly Grimes, lighting design by Justin Townsend, and sound design by Palmer Heffernan. The Production Stage Manager was Jennifer Khan. The cast was as follows:

LIZ EBERWINE . . . . Mary Wiseman

LILY EBERWINE . . . . .Emily Lyons

BERNIE HOLLIS . . . . Ashley Austin Morris

JAKE/CHARLES/MYRON . . . . .Justin Long

CECILIA EBERWINE . . . . Connie Ray

BOBBY EBERWINE . . . . .Andrew Weems

CHARACTERS

LIZ EBERWINE – F, twenty-nine years old. Southern. Determined to maintain a sunny disposition and to shield her daughter, Lily, from life's tougher realities.

LILY EBERWINE – F, six years old. Liz's outgoing, curious, and playful daughter. Also southern.

BERNIE HOLLIS – F, thirty-two years old. Liz's older sister. Born and raised in Mississippi, but relocated herself to New York when she was eighteen. The life of the party, up for anything…as long as she doesn't have to stay too long. Bernie has some bad tattoos. Wild Spring Breaks, Boone's Farm wine products, and throw-down games of truth or dare have left their mark.

JAKE/CHARLES/MYRON – M, thirty-ish years old.

> **JAKE** is from Boston and is a personal trainer. A go-getter and ready to transform your life.
>
> **CHARLES** is from Upstate New York and lives in Brooklyn. He is really into the Brooklyn artisanal scene and is just cool as shit.
>
> **MYRON** is an old-fashioned romantic. A jazz trumpet player who pays his bills playing in the orchestra of *Wicked*.

CECILIA EBERWINE – F, fifty-five years old. Liz's mother-in-law. A southern belle through and through. A spark plug, but always polite. The boss, never without her pearls.

BOBBY EBERWINE – M, fifty-five years old. Liz's father-in-law and southern. A teddy bear. A funny, funny man with a great laugh and a big heart.

SETTING

Brooklyn, NY

TIME

The Present

Scene One

(Lights up on **LIZ** *and* **BERNIE** *in their Brooklyn Heights apartment.)*

LIZ. Tragedy. Tragic events have occurred, and my story will be forever classified by them. The genre is set. The genre is tragedy. Once Anna Karenina throws herself under the train, she's not gonna get up, brush herself off, and have another chance at life. No! It's a tragedy. That's it. It will always end with the reader putting the book down with a lump in their throat, as they sigh and say, "What a tragedy. My God. It is just so tragic."

BERNIE. Lizzy?

LIZ. What?

BERNIE. All it asks is: "What is the first thing that people usually notice about you?"

LIZ. That is the first thing. Tragedy.

BERNIE. You can't put that on an OkCupid profile, girl.

LIZ. Might as well be real clear about it from the get-go.

BERNIE. I think something like "my smile" or "my accent" would work.

LIZ. People see me: BOOM! Pity hits them like a speeding bullet.

BERNIE. I'm just gonna write "smile." "Do you consider God to be an important part of your life?"

LIZ. That's none of their business!

BERNIE. It's just so that they can try to match you with someone who is like you. No! Put that book down and let's have fun!

LIZ. This book is fun!

BERNIE. Liz. Your romance novels aren't gonna keep you warm at night. Nor are they able to provide oral satisfaction.

LIZ. I think some oral is gonna happen in this book, actually. I have a feeling.

BERNIE. I don't even know how to respond to that.

LIZ. Oh shoot! I need to start dinner. Taco Tuesday.

BERNIE. No Tac Tues for me. Enshantay has a show.

LIZ. Oooh, fun!

BERNIE. Y'all should come with me!

LIZ. I am not bringing a six-year-old to a drag show in the West Village.

BERNIE. She's almost seven.

LIZ. Maybe when she's ten.

BERNIE. Eight.

LIZ. Nine.

BERNIE. Deal. We are killing this parent thing! Shouldn't Lily be home by now?

LIZ. Indigo's mom should have her here soon. They took Spaghetti to the dog run.

> (**LIZ** *begins prepping dinner.* **BERNIE** *takes out a one-hitter, lights it, and smokes.*)

Girl! Lily is about to walk through that door.

BERNIE. But she's not here now.

> (**LIZ** *begins spraying air freshener.*)

LIZ. I've asked you not to smoke pot in my house.

BERNIE. Our house.

LIZ. I've asked you.

BERNIE. I forgot.

LILY. *(Offstage.)* Mama! Spaghetti is pooping all over the front mat!

BERNIE. That dog is messed up, girl. You need to get / him checked.

LIZ. I'm taking him to the vet on Wednesday.

(LIZ runs out the front door. BERNIE reaches for her wine, knocks it over so that it spills. She takes an afghan from the couch, wipes up the spill with it, and folds the afghan so that the wine stain is hidden.)

(Offstage.) Bye Indigo! Thanks, Carol. We have a vet appointment on Wednesday.

(LILY runs in.)

LILY. Bonjour, Silly Aunt Bernie.

BERNIE. Bonjour, Niece Lily Dilly.

(They stop play-pretending sophisticated French ladies, and BERNIE rushes LILY.)

I'm so happy you're home! I LOVE MY DILLY!

LILY. I LOVE MY SILLY!

(LIZ comes in, carrying a leash.)

BERNIE. So Spaghetti straight-up dirty diarrhea'd all over the neighborhood?

LILY. Yeah!

LIZ. I took him around back to the garden, we have / a vet –

BERNIE. What did it look like?

LILY. Pudding! Chocolate pudding!

LIZ. Y'all. That's a wrap on the poop talk. How was school, Dill?

LILY. At recess, I swung as high as the trees! If I fell out of the swing I would have died! I would have died like Daddy!

LIZ. Lily. You're not gonna die from the swings.

LILY. Uh-huh! I was so high that –

LIZ. Baby, don't play like you're gonna fall from the swings, okay?

LILY. I would be dead!

LIZ. Go wash your hands and put your stuff away, please ma'am.

BERNIE. What are you gonna wear for Taco Tuesday?

LILY. I don't know.

BERNIE. I'm thinking I would like to see some Pirate-Beyoncé-Fiesta realness.

LILY. WORD!

>   (**LILY** *runs to her room.*)

BERNIE. We gotta talk to Lily about the reality of death.

LIZ. She's six.

BERNIE. She's confused.

LIZ. I'm sure she is, I'm confused too!

BERNIE. It's getting worse.

LIZ. Can we talk about this later?

BERNIE. Yesterday, when we were walking home, she asked me what she should wear on her first day of Heaven. I told her she should probably go with something gold. I was about to tell her that there's actually no such thing as Heaven, but Spaghetti exploded all over the sidewalk and I didn't have any bags so we had to make a run for it.

LIZ. Wait. Bernie, you can't tell her –

BERNIE. Girl, she talks about dying more and more. We just need to sit down / and talk to her.

>   (**LILY** *runs back in, serving some Pirate-Beyoncé-Fiesta realness.*)

LILY. Taco Tuesday!

BERNIE. DAYUM. Looks like I'm gonna have to pull out the sombrero! I must join you in this Fiesta Eleganza Extravaganza!

LIZ. You're gonna miss Enshantay's show, Bernie?

BERNIE. She'll live.

LILY Too bad for her. Dying rules!

>   (*Beat. The sisters share a look.*)

BERNIE. You know what rules? Working that runway. Five-six-seven-eight.

(**LILY** *begins working the runway.*)

Girl, you better work! Look at all that charisma, uniqueness, nerve and talent!

LIZ. Oh yes, girl!

BERNIE. Dilly, you are sickening! Liz, can you even believe how amazing this creature is?

LIZ. No. I really can't.

Scene Two

*(**LIZ** finishes dishes from Taco Tuesday, **BERNIE** pours wine. She wears a sombrero.)*

BERNIE. I was sitting on this fire escape, Manhattan below me, smoking a cigarette, and I kept glancing into the bedroom to see this guy, John (?). DAYUM. He was this strong, handsome man. Huuuuge D.

LIZ. Girl.

BERNIE. And get this: he was an abstract oil painter.

*(She waits for **LIZ** to be impressed. Nothing.)*

We had just knocked boots four – four and a half times – in two hours. I had just moved to New York City. Girl, it was like Rent The Musical.

LIZ. Wait. Really?!

BERNIE. Yeah, girl. I sat on that fire escape, watching John (?) breathe his first few falling asleep breaths and the most incredible feeling hit me. The feeling of deep, bottomless freedom. It just smacked me right in the face and I felt so…happy. Then, I finished my cig, snuck back inside, put my clothes on, left his apartment, went to Gray's Papaya, housed a corn dog, and walked around New York until the sun came up. Now, that: THAT is romance.

LIZ. But girl, what does the story look like in ten years? It's not gonna be romantic when you're a fifty-year-old woman having a one-night / stand –

BERNIE. Easy! In ten years I will be *forty-two*. So / relax.

LIZ. – and smoking alone on a dingy fire escape as you stare at yet another old man you poured everything you had left into, snoring himself to sleep.

BERNIE. I might be dead in ten years.

LIZ. Girl.

BERNIE. Who knows? I might be!

LIZ. Please don't say that.

BERNIE. Shit. I'm sorry, girl. I just mean…you know, get it while you can. Sorry.

LIZ. Should I be worried?

BERNIE. About what?

LIZ. Lily wanting to be dead.

BERNIE. We just need to talk to her.

LIZ. She sleeps with his hat. Bradley's baseball hat. His blue Ole Miss hat.

BERNIE. I think that's okay.

LIZ. It still has blood on it. They gave it to me at the police station. A couple of nights later, I'm putting Lily to bed, and I see it under her covers. She had taken it out of my purse. I tried to take it away from her but she shrieked and sobbed. I told her she could keep it but that I had to wash it. I went to put it in the machine and the same thing: screaming, sobbing. It's covered in blood, it's filthy, but I can't wash it.

BERNIE. It doesn't have to be washed. And you don't have to talk to her about death, sorry I've been making a big deal about her saying that stuff.

LIZ. Well, it could be a big deal. I don't know.

BERNIE. Whatever it is we'll handle it.

LIZ. You didn't want to see that magician again?

BERNIE. What?

LIZ. John.

BERNIE. He's not a magician. He's an abstract oil painter. I have never slept with a magician.

LIZ. You didn't want to see him again? I mean, he has a huge D, right?

BERNIE. A D's just a D, girl.

LIZ. Seeing him twice doesn't mean you have to marry him.

BERNIE. Stay in one thing too long and wake up ten years later, sweaty and panicked with "How did I get here and how the fuck do I get out?!" screeching through your head.

LIZ. How did I get here, Bernie?

BERNIE. I wasn't talking about you, Liz. You know that.

LIZ. I am twenty-nine with a six-year-old daughter and I just moved to a new city where I know no one. Oh, and I am a WIDOW. I am a WIDOW. How did I get here?

BERNIE. Your life got yanked away from you. And now you are grabbing it by the balls and yanking it back. That's how you got here. Oh, shit! I totally forgot! I got you a little sumthin' sumthin'.

(**BERNIE** *pulls a book out of her purse.*)

LIZ. *Writing a Romance Novel for Dummies.*

BERNIE. Girl, you could write! This is your chance to –

LIZ. I'm not a writer / Bernie.

BERNIE. You are obsessed with romance novels! You are obsessed with books!

LIZ. Just because I like to read, doesn't mean I'm a writer.

BERNIE. This place will show you that there are other options besides wife and mother.

LIZ. I like being a wife and a mother.

BERNIE. Sure. But you got a big ol' life ahead of you!

LIZ. That right?

BERNIE. A big ol' life in a pimpin-ass brownstone that your rich in-laws paid for. We're like, *MTV Cribs* up in here, girl. It doesn't get much better than this.

LIZ. My husband died six months ago.

BERNIE. I just mean…this is a straight-up fresh start. You are in a city of strangers. You get to be whoever the hell you want. Let's finish your OkCupid profile, girl.

LIZ. I love ya, but I'm not gonna be going on anything close to a date.

BERNIE. Do not say that! That's why you're here!

LIZ. I didn't move up to –

BERNIE. I am home every night by nine to help you put Lily to bed. The least you could do for me is to go ahead and get on that party train. You are young, you are gorgeous, you have got to get out there! It'll be a nice distraction, you'll walk away with some funny stories, maybe get laid.

LIZ. Girl, I can't just "get laid."

BERNIE. Uh, yeah you can. Get out there. Make some mistakes.

LIZ. You realize that I have not gone on a date. Not ever.

BERNIE. We went to *Save the Last Dance* with the DeVeronica brothers in junior high. Mid-movie, you ran to the bathroom, cried to me in the stall that you couldn't french Jeff DeVeronica because you "didn't want to be another trophy in his case."

LIZ. He was frenching everybody! He was the lothario of our seventh-grade class!

BERNIE. "I don't want to be another trophy in his case."

LIZ. Girl, the *Save the Last Dance* experience doesn't count as a date.

BERNIE. Honestly, not much does these days.

LIZ. Bradley and I became a couple when I was fifteen. How do I even…and on the internet?!

BERNIE. Girl, everybody does it on the net. I'm not saying get into a relationship, you know how I feel about those. I just want you to have fun. You could go to ethnic restaurants, get dressed up, fix your hair real cute.

LIZ. I could…

BERNIE. What?

LIZ. Buy some earrings?

BERNIE. Yes, girl!

LIZ. Some big ones?

BERNIE. Oh, big gold hoop earrings, you little slut! Let the good times roll! Best way to get over a man is to get under a new one!

LIZ. Girl!

BERNIE. Sorry.

LIZ. You can't use that quote when you are talking about my dead husband!

BERNIE. Right when it came out it felt wrong.

LIZ. Good Lord.

BERNIE. Sorry.

LIZ. You are out of control.

BERNIE. Sorry. See? Isn't this better than being in that haunted-ass town? Down there with Bradley's parents all up on your nuts.

LIZ. CeeCee and Papa Bobby were just trying to help. They weren't all up on my…nuts.

(*Beat.*)

Thank you.

BERNIE. For what?

LIZ. The book. And everything. I do think Lily is happy here.

BERNIE. We're gonna be kick-ass parents. In this together. But girl, we're not gonna get *Grey Gardens* up in here.

LIZ. No. No *Grey Gardens*.

BERNIE. We're gonna have fun.

LIZ. We are gonna have fun. But right now I'm going to bed.

BERNIE. I'm coming with you.

LIZ. Girl, you have to sleep in your own room. You kicked me so hard in your sleep last night.

BERNIE. We're staying up in bed and finishing your OkCupid profile. We can eat fruit roll-ups and check out all the guys that you're gonna bang.

LIZ. Those fruit roll-ups are for Lily to take to school for snack time.

BERNIE. She needs to learn to share.

LIZ. Okay. But you can't sleep naked.

BERNIE. It's the only way!

LIZ. At least put on some underwear this time, girl.

BERNIE. Girl, that's the whole point of sleeping naked. Things need to air out. Might want to try it. Especially since you 'bout to get your freak on!

LIZ. I am not 'bout to get my freak on!

BERNIE. Girl, you 'bout to get freak nasty up in this club!

LIZ. What club?! I'm not going to a club!

BERNIE. It's just a saying. I'm saying like, you're gonna have sex soon.

LIZ. In a club?!

BERNIE. There is no actual club. It's just a saying. Do you know what a saying is?

LIZ. Yes. I know what a saying is. Girl.

*(Beat. **LIZ** gives a mischievous smirk.)*

You get the laptop, I'll get the fruit roll-ups. Let's get this party started.

Scene Three

(The phone rings. **LILY** *answers it.)*

LILY. Hello? Hey CeeCee! Hey Papa Bobby! …Yeah! …Sorry, yes ma'am! …Me and Bernie are gonna make up dance routines all night because Mama is going out! Enshantay is coming over, too! He's a man but he wears dresses at nighttime.

> *(***LIZ*** *enters, dressed up, with big gold hoop earrings.)*

LIZ. Who is it, Dill?

LILY. CeeCee and Papa Bobby! CeeCee wants to know where you are going.

LIZ. Uh, a thing for your school.

> *(***LIZ*** *gets everything ready before she leaves for the night: labeling things in the fridge, writing down instructions, etc.)*

LILY. Something for my school…CeeCee wants to know what kind of school has a thing at seven p.m. on a Thursday?

LIZ. Tell her it's a parents' get-together to talk about… safety.

LILY. It's a parents' get-together to talk about safety… CeeCee wants to know if there are problems with safety at my school?

LIZ. No. Your school is very safe.

LILY. My school is very safe…CeeCee wants to know what Aunt Bernie is going to cook me for dinner because she wasn't aware that Aunt Bernie knew how to use an oven.

> *(***LIZ*** *takes the phone.)*

LIZ. Lasagna. I made it earlier and she just has to pop it in the microwave…Yes, we have a smoke detector. Can we call y'all back…I changed the batteries two days ago… Lithium. Lithium batteries. I gotta get going –

LILY. I miss y'all!

LIZ. Yes, she does…No ma'am, not in the next couple of weeks. Well, because Lily just started her new and extremely safe school…I know you do…Y'all, we will call –

>   (**LIZ** *looks at* **LILY***'s outfit and gives her in-laws a description.*)

A blue dress with pink flowers on it. Right now, pigtails. I have to run. Okay, talk soon…Love you, too.

>   (**LIZ** *hangs up the phone.*)

Now, I want you in bed by / nine o'clock.

>   (**BERNIE** *flings open the front door, carrying bottles of wine.*)

BERNIE. Dilly, are you ready for the most fabulous night of your life?

LILY. Yes, ma'am!

BERNIE. Lillian Hollis Eberwine. What did I say about that?

LILY. Sorry. Yaaaasss, GIRL.

BERNIE. We're back on the "ma'am and sir" shit, Liz?

LIZ. Watch your language and she was just on the phone with CeeCee.

BERNIE. Freaking Southern Hospitality Nazi.

LILY. What's a Nazi?

BERNIE. What's for dinner, Mama?

LIZ. Lasagna. Just pop it –

BERNIE. Damn. I was hoping you made green bean casserole. I was craving that GBC. Nice earrings.

LIZ. Heat it on high for –

BERNIE. Your mama looks hot, Dill. Hot in a Ann Taylor Loft kind of way, but hot. You gotta go, girl. It's almost seven.

LIZ. Oh goodness. Okay. Are you sure I should go?

BERNIE. We need you to go so that we can stretch before Enshantay gets here and starts teaching us combinations.

LIZ. Bernie, I can't do this. I'm gonna cancel.

BERNIE. Get out of this house.

LILY. Bye, Mama!

LIZ. Bye, baby. Don't stay up past / nine p.m.

BERNIE. If you aren't coming home just text / me.

LIZ. Girl, I am coming / home.

BERNIE. Okay, but just text me like a winky face and I'll know that you aren't / coming back.

LIZ. You are out of control. / I love you, Dill!

LILY. I love you, too!

BERNIE. *(Pushing* **LIZ** *out.)* Bye, girl!

Scene Four

*(**LIZ** enters a bar, looks around, and nervously walks up to a handsome, sporty man.)*

LIZ. Jake?

JAKE. Liz?

LIZ. Hi!

JAKE. Awesome. You're gorgeous.

LIZ. Oh. Thank you.

JAKE. Have a seat.

LIZ. Okay.

JAKE. And how are you today?

LIZ. I'm good. Not too much of a crazy day. And you?

JAKE. Stellar day. I had a few clients, no complaints.

LIZ. You're a personal trainer? That's what your thingy said.

JAKE. My thingy?

LIZ. Your profile.

JAKE. Right. That thingy.

LIZ. That profile thingy.

JAKE. Not the other thingy?

LIZ. What?

JAKE. Joke. I was making a joke.

LIZ. Oh.

*(**LIZ** laughs at the "joke." It's awkward.)*

It must be interesting. Being a personal trainer.

JAKE. Best job ever. What is it that you do? Your profile thingy was pretty vague. You didn't answer half the questions.

LIZ. Those questions are crazy!

JAKE. Not questions like "What is your profession?" So?

LIZ. I'm...figuring it out.

JAKE. Right, right. A time of transition?

LIZ. Like, professionally speaking?

JAKE. Yeah.

LIZ. Yes. A time of transition. I'm in between things.

JAKE. What is it that you want to do?

LIZ. With my career?

JAKE. With your life! What's your passion?

LIZ. I don't really…

JAKE. Want to do something with your life? Uh-oh!

LIZ. No, that's not…um.

JAKE. What do you live for?

LIZ. Like, a profession? What profession do I live for?

JAKE. Your calling. Your passion. Isn't that why everyone in this city gets up in the morning? Isn't that why you get up in the morning? For your calling?

(Beat.)

LIZ. Yes.

JAKE. So, what is it?

LIZ. I want…I want to be a writer.

JAKE. No shit?

LIZ. I love to read, so I want to be a writer. I want to write novels.

JAKE. What kind of novels do you want to write?

LIZ. I want to write romance novels.

JAKE. Like, Fabio type shit?

LIZ. Yes. Romance Novels.

JAKE. That is the coolest thing I have ever heard.

LIZ. You're making fun of me!

JAKE. I'm not! That is cool! You must be wicked smart. I have never met anyone who does that.

LIZ. Well, I just want to do it, I don't actually do it.

JAKE. But you're going to. When we go on our next date, I want you to have started your first romance novel. I want you to have written fifteen pages. Deal?

LIZ. Wow, you really are a personal trainer.

JAKE. It's who I am.

LIZ. Did you always want to be...to do that with your life?

JAKE. That is actually a really great question. You know, what I really wanted was to be a professional hockey player. Played hockey my whole life, tore my ACL and had to stop.

LIZ. Oh, dear.

JAKE. Yeah. It was tough. A really tough time.

LIZ. I'm sorry.

JAKE. Don't be. Because it all turned out okay, you know? I was able to discover my passion for personal training. Here's the thing, Liz: sometimes life throws you a curve ball and you just gotta roll with the punches.

LIZ. Right.

JAKE. Lemons to lemonade.

LIZ. Uh-huh.

JAKE. Basically, what I'm saying is: You gotta take something bad, and try to make something / good –

LIZ. Yeah, no, I got it.

JAKE. So, you're southern?

LIZ. You can tell?

JAKE. Your accent was the first thing I noticed!

LIZ. Oh, yeah?

JAKE. Yeah. You got a pretty killer smile, too.

LIZ. Thank you. You got a bit of an accent yourself, sir.

JAKE. Boston, born and raised! How do you like them apples?

(They laugh too long and too hard at his joke.)

So, why New York?

LIZ. Uh. So I can follow my dreams of being a writer.

JAKE. Can't you write anywhere?

LIZ. Sure, but...fresh start. I guess I needed a change.

JAKE. From what?

LIZ. It's a long story.

JAKE. I'm listening. Tell it to me like a romance novel!

LIZ. What?

JAKE. Your story.

LIZ. You want me to tell my story…like a romance novel?

JAKE. Yeah, let's see your skills!

LIZ. Umm, I can't just…

JAKE. YOU GOT THIS, L!

LIZ. There is a very specific formula that romance novels follow, so it's tricky.

JAKE. For real? There's a formula?

LIZ. Yeah, the rules are pretty much laid out for you.

JAKE. Hit me.

LIZ. Well, the beginning of a novel has to follow a certain mold to captivate the reader.

JAKE. Okay, so page one of how Liz – what is your last name?

LIZ. Eberwine.

JAKE. Okay, page one of the "Liz Eberwine Moves To New York City" story.

LIZ. I can't do it when I am on the spot like this!

JAKE. Alright, then, I'm gonna give it a shot. Lead by example. Here goes: Liz leaned against her porch railing, used her bandana to wipe beads of sweat off her chest and then tucked it into the back pocket of her tiny, ripped up, cut-off jean shorts –

LIZ. Uh –

JAKE. She could feel the wet grass beneath her bare feet –

LIZ. I thought I was standing on a porch –

JAKE. And even though there were only crickets chirping, she could hear the sounds of New York City calling her name, luring her in…not unlike Odysseus and the Sirens of the sea.

LIZ. Wow.

JAKE. Sick line. Well done, Jake. Okay. One Tuesday the volume of the Sirens' song was particularly high. She could no longer stand it! She hitched a ride to the train station, and used all of her savings for a one-way ticket to New York City. Am I getting it?

LIZ. I just needed a change. Um. I've never been to Boston. I would love to see it.

JAKE. I could show you around.

LIZ. Ha! Yeah. No. Yeah, that sounds great.

JAKE. I like your earrings.

LIZ. Thanks.

JAKE. They're fun.

(JAKE *smiles.* LIZ *does, too.*)

Scene Five

(Later that night. **BERNIE** *sits on the couch, drinking wine and playing with* **LILY***'s dolls.* **LILY** *is cuddled up next to her, asleep in a black leather jacket and a black biker hat. The house is a mess.)*

*(***LIZ*** enters.)*

BERNIE. You're already back?!

LIZ. Shhh! How was it? How's Lily?

BERNIE. Dill and Enshantay made up dance routines to every song on Janet Jackson's *Design of a Decade* album and had me critique them.

LIZ. Oh, wow.

BERNIE. Lily is very flexible. Homegirl has got legs for days. The last move of every dance was Dilly and Enshantay doing a slow-motion split. Quite effective. Then she fell asleep, Enshantay went back to Manhattan, and I just cleaned up a big pile of Spaghetti's shit off your Pottery Barn rug. That dog is FUCKED.

LIZ. Shhhh! We have a vet appointment on Wednesday.

*(***LIZ*** begins to quietly clean the house.)*

BERNIE. Girl?

LIZ. What?

BERNIE. You're being real stingy with the mustard.

LIZ. What are you talking / about?

BERNIE. Girl, tell me about Jake! Give me the deets!

LIZ. It was good.

BERNIE. How?! What happened?!

LIZ. We had drinks and apps, it was good!

BERNIE. Did y'all french?

LIZ. No!

BERNIE. Hold hands?

LIZ. No!

BERNIE. Was it flirty, though?

LIZ. Maybe…I don't know.

BERNIE. Come on, girl!

LIZ. Yeah girl, I think there was some flirting happening.

BERNIE. You. Dirty. Fucking. Slut.

LIZ. Shhhh! Bernie!

BERNIE. You had fun?

LIZ. I think so…

BERNIE. When are y'all gonna get more drinks and apps?

LIZ. We'll see.

BERNIE. Girl, he's dumb?

LIZ. No.

BERNIE. A little cross-eyed?

LIZ. No.

BERNIE. There was something about his picture that made me wonder if he might be a little cross-eyed in person, like sort of retarded.

LIZ. That word, Bernie! He's great. Just, we'll see.

BERNIE. That's right! This is straight-up casual dating. No need to think about what's next. But you had fun?

LIZ. Yes, girl. I had fun.

BERNIE. Was he psyched to be on a date with a total MILF?

LIZ. What?

BERNIE. Was he freaked out about Lily?

LIZ. No…no.

BERNIE. How were his teeth?

LIZ. I'm gonna put her in bed.

BERNIE. I'm going to the store. We need some Korbel to celebrate Stella gettin' her groove back!

LIZ. What? Bernie we do not –

(**BERNIE** *is at the front door.*)

BERNIE. Mama's back on the market! Can I get a "What, what!"

(**BERNIE** *is out the door.* **LIZ** *walks to* **LILY** *and softly kisses her cheek.*)

LILY. Mama?

LIZ. Hey, Dill. Let's get you to bed. Wow. I love your costume.

LILY. I'm gonna wear this to Heaven.

LIZ. …

LILY. Bernie smokes cigarettes.

LIZ. You saw her smoking?

LILY. …

LIZ. Grown-ups are weird, huh, Dill? Dilly?

> (**LILY** *has fallen asleep in* **LIZ**'s *arms. A moment passes.*)

Night, night, baby. I love you as big as the sky.

Scene Six

(LIZ at the bar, on a date with CHARLES.)

LIZ. It's true! Romance is the best-selling genre in all fiction. So, here are the rules: you gotta have a sympathetic heroine, a strong, irresistible hero; a believable plot, and a happily-ever-after ending. And you have to deliver because romance readers know what they want and expect you to give it to them.

CHARLES. So, no surprises?

LIZ. There can be some surprises as long as there is a happy ending. The ultimate expectation every reader has when reading a romance novel is that it will end with the hero and heroine planning to spend their lives together and face any future trials as one.

CHARLES. How many have you written?

LIZ. Uh, two are published, but I've written more. Than two.

CHARLES. I'll have to pick one up.

LIZ. Oh, no –

CHARLES. Oh. Yes.

LIZ. I write under an alias. I don't use my real name. So. You can't find them.

CHARLES. What is your alias?

LIZ. I'm not telling you! That's the whole point of an alias: anonymity. This drink is delicious! Charles, isn't that what you do? Your profile said that you are a mixologist?

CHARLES. I am now, but I am gonna open my own place soon. But no fancy shit. It's gonna be really simple and just fucking cool as shit.

LIZ. Oh, cool.

CHARLES. It's gonna be called "Whiskey and Cake."

LIZ. That's a great name for a bar.

CHARLES. Well, the tits thing is: that's all we're gonna serve.

LIZ. What?

CHARLES. Whiskey and cake.

LIZ. Like cake, cake?

CHARLES. Yeah, we're gonna have a few fucking delectable cakes on display on some silver, like, antique fancy trays and shit and then we are just gonna have whiskey behind the bar.

LIZ. Can you mix in anything with your whiskey, like a Diet / Coke or something?

CHARLES. No mixers. Neat or on the rocks. That's it. Whiskey and Cake. I think it's gonna be fucking huge. We're getting back to the basics. People want that.

> *(Pause. It feels like an awkward silence to* **LIZ**, *but not to* **CHARLES**.*)*

This bar is a little bougie. Right?

LIZ. Uhh, yeah…?

CHARLES. My buddy is hosting bingo at his bar a few blocks over, wanna go check it out?

LIZ. I should get home.

CHARLES. It's Saturday. The night is young, Liz.

LIZ. I have a deadline.

CHARLES. Alright then. I'll walk you home?

LIZ. Go play bingo! I'm fine!

CHARLES. I'll walk you. Where do you live?

LIZ. Brooklyn Heights.

CHARLES. Roommates?

LIZ. Um, two.

CHARLES. You gonna go home and tell them you met the man of your dreams tonight?

LIZ. Oh, yeah. I'm gonna tell them that you are about to be the next big thing in the NYC cocktail scene.

CHARLES. Right on. But, like, don't say too much.

LIZ. Operation Whiskey and Cake is purely confidential.

> *(They laugh for a bit.)*

CHARLES. No, but seriously, could you not say anything to anyone about it?

LIZ. Oh. Yeah. Yes.

CHARLES. You sure I can't walk you home?

LIZ. I like to walk by myself, I can think about things.

CHARLES. Your next novel?

LIZ. Yes.

CHARLES. I gotta say.

> *(Pause.)*

LIZ. What?

CHARLES. What?

LIZ. You were gonna say / something –

CHARLES. Right, right. It's sexy. Your profession. It's weird and funny and real fucking sexy.

LIZ. Thank…um, thank you. Thanks.

CHARLES. Thank YOU.

LIZ. You're welcome (?).

CHARLES. If you won't let me walk you home, let's pretend this is your front stoop. These bar stools are the steps and we are sitting on them and you are just about to get up and go inside.

LIZ. Um. Okay.

CHARLES. And then I stop you.

LIZ. Okay.

CHARLES. And then I kiss you.

> *(**CHARLES** kisses **LIZ**.)*

LIZ. Okay. Awesome.

> *(**CHARLES** kisses **LIZ** again.)*

We're…at the bar. I can't…kiss at the bar.

CHARLES. We don't have to stay at the bar.

LIZ. I have to…my deadline.

CHARLES. Sexy. You're leaving me to go write. I respect that and I think it is very. Fucking. Hot.

LIZ. What is?

CHARLES. Your passion for your work. It's a turn-on. You turn me on, Liz.

*(**CHARLES** stares at **LIZ**.)*

CHARLES. Get the fuck out of here. Go. Write.
LIZ. Right. Okay. Goodnight.
CHARLES. Goodnight, Liz.

Scene Seven

(Later that night. **BERNIE** *and* **LILY** *are cuddled on the couch. Both have the same side ponytail, the same blue eyeshadow.* **LIZ** *walks in.)*

LILY. Mama! We're watching *Dirty Dancing*!

LIZ. Bernie, she can't watch *Dirty Dancing*!

BERNIE. It's a kids' movie, *Dirty Dancing*!

LILY. They go like this!

*(***LILY*** *begins doing sexual dance moves.)*

BERNIE. Girl, we've got a dancer on our hands.

LIZ. Lily, stop it. Stop dancing like that.

LILY. Check out this move!

*(***LILY*** *begins doing another suggestive move.)*

LIZ. Lily, STOP!

BERNIE. Dill, go brush your teeth and come back in your new nightgown?

*(***LILY*** *smiles and dashes to her room.)*

LIZ. Lily can't do that, Bernie.

BERNIE. She was expressing herself through movement.

LIZ. *Dirty Dancing* is an R-rated movie.

BERNIE. It's nothing! They just dance.

LIZ. Girl, that Rockette gets an abortion!

BERNIE. There are no Rockettes in *Dirty Dancing*!

LIZ. Penny! Penny was a Rockette before she started teaching dance at / the resort.

BERNIE. I didn't know that. Do they talk about Penny being a former / Rockette?

LIZ. Yes. Please, no R-rated movies.

BERNIE. Lily is mature.

LIZ. Lily is six.

BERNIE. Girl, do you honestly think Lily digs movies made for six-year-olds?

LIZ. I honestly do. Because she is six!

BERNIE. She's almost seven. So.

LIZ. Bernie.

BERNIE. Fine. No more *Dirty D.*

LIZ. Thank you.

>   *(Pause.)*

>   He kissed me.

BERNIE. Shut the fuck up!

LIZ. Shhhh!

BERNIE. Was it a french?

LIZ. Yes! At the bar! Girl, people were around!

BERNIE. Oh shit, girl. Everyone is gonna be talking about it.

LIZ. What?

BERNIE. Girl, I'm a little concerned about your reputation. People / are gonna –

LIZ. Are you serious?

BERNIE. No! This is Brooklyn. This isn't Holly Grove!

LIZ. It's okay? I'm not doing anything wrong?

BERNIE. What are you talking about?

LIZ. It's okay? Right? It's fine?

BERNIE. Oh my God. This is the only person that you've ever kissed.

LIZ. Other than Bradley.

BERNIE. In your whole life. *(Putting her arms around* **LIZ**.*)* You're doing great, Liz.

LIZ. Bernie. It was fun.

BERNIE. Yeah, girl?

LIZ. Yeah, girl.

BERNIE. Was he a good kisser?

LIZ. I think so. He's…

BERNIE. What?

LIZ. Sexy (?).

(BERNIE and LIZ transform into schoolgirls.)

BERNIE. Yeah?! Girl, was it passionate?

LIZ. It was. And…

BERNIE. What?

LIZ. Girl, he grabbed my butt!

BERNIE. Shut. Up.

LIZ. I think he wanted to like –

BERNIE. FUCK?

LIZ. Girl!

BERNIE. Oh my God, he totally wanted to bone you!

LIZ. Girl!

BERNIE. What? You're a straight-up MILF!

LIZ. He said I was hot!

BERNIE. *(A cheer.)* H-O-T-T-O-G-O, bitch you're straight-up hot to go! Woo! Woo! Hot to go!

LIZ. He like, grabbed my face / and just –

BERNIE. With his big, strong, man / hands.

LIZ. Like, kissed me.

BERNIE. So fun!

LIZ. Yeah, and I don't even like him, but it was fun!

BERNIE. Look at you, you little fun and sexy mama! Who's a sexy mama? Who-who-who?

> *(LIZ and BERNIE begin dancing and singing "Who's a sexy mama?" It's raunchy and young. They don't see LILY sneak in and watch them. She is wearing a big t-shirt with "Bustin' Loose" printed on it. LILY begins to quietly dirty dance.)*

LILY. Who's a sexy mama? Who-who-who?

> *(LIZ and BERNIE freeze and see LILY singing and dancing. BERNIE looks at LIZ nervously. LIZ begins to laugh. Then, she laughs harder.)*

Scene Eight

(**LIZ** *is on a date with* **MYRON**. *They drink coffee on a park bench.*)

LIZ. Claire's mother dies when Claire is four and her father works night and day. It's just Claire and her older sister, Franny. The two sisters raise each other and for a long time, it's just them in their own little world. Taking care of each other, raising each another.

MYRON. Get to the love story!

LIZ. Right, right. Gabe was raised under different circumstances: his father is a lawyer and his mother is an eminent figure in southern society.

MYRON. So, Claire and Gabe were an unlikely pair.

LIZ. Exactly. But on his ninth birthday while playing catch in his front yard, Gabe sees Claire for the first time. She's on her bicycle and she rides past him without holding on to her handlebars. He's done for.

MYRON. She's a free spirit. Gabe can't resist a free spirit.

LIZ. Are you making fun of my novel?

MYRON. No, continue. I'm sorry. Please.

LIZ. All through elementary school, junior high; he chases after her, but she doesn't give him the time of day.

MYRON. Why not? He sounds great: he's rich, he plays catch.

LIZ. Because Claire and Franny are in their own bubble. They can't see past one another. For Claire to play pretend with someone else, to go on a date with someone, to love someone…it felt like…she couldn't leave her sister's side.

MYRON. Sure she could.

LIZ. Their mother had died, their dad wasn't around. They were each other's foundation. You get that. I lay that out in the book. The complications.

MYRON. Okay.

LIZ. So, because they had no one looking out for them and Franny had a, um, wild streak; the girls were getting into a lot of trouble.

MYRON. Ooh, like what?

LIZ. You name it. Franny was up for anything. And Claire did whatever her big sister did. When Claire was fifteen, the girls get arrested for shoplifting. They're too scared to call their father, so Claire calls Gabe. Gabe bails them out. He drives them home, Franny gets out of the truck, and Gabe yells at Claire. He tells her that she is an idiot. Then he takes off his blue baseball hat, swoops in, and kisses her. He's mad and excited and protective. Right then and there in the front seat of that Dodge Ram, Claire falls in love.

MYRON. They tear each others clothes off and have animalistic / acrobatic –

LIZ. No! They're just fifteen! They wait!

MYRON. I thought romance novels were steamy! A lot of shirts being ripped open –

LIZ. With Gabe's help, Claire turns her life around. They become inseparable: best friends, passionate lovers, the prize couple of that small Mississippi town. They fall more and more in love with each day that passes.

MYRON. What about Franny?

LIZ. Um. She finds her way. She has her own life and figures out –

MYRON. Does the book ever come back to her?

LIZ. It's a romance novel! It's about Claire and Gabe.

MYRON. Alright, alright. Franny just disappears –

LIZ. She doesn't disappear, the book just moves on to –

MYRON. Claire and Gabe. Right. Okay. Onwards.

LIZ. They get married. Claire gives birth to a beautiful baby girl. It is a dream life. They hold hands and kiss at the movies. They eat pancakes and spray each other with garden hoses and go to baseball games and when it's time to go to sleep they feel tired and sunburned and full. Every day, Gabe says to Claire: "I love you as big as the sky." Then, one day, a Sunday, Gabe is killed in a horrific car accident. That's how it ends.

MYRON. Wait. What?

LIZ. I think I should change it.

MYRON. I just wasn't expecting that...the car accident.

LIZ. Right, it can't be bleak.

MYRON. Bleak can be interesting.

LIZ. Not for romance novels. They must have a happy ending.

MYRON. That's a rule?

LIZ. For traditional romance novels, yes. Now, if you're writing Chick Lit –

MYRON. Chick Lit?

LIZ. Chick Lit is heroine-focused and a happily ever after ending isn't required and is often pointedly avoided. I don't write Chick Lit.

MYRON. So, do you have another idea for the ending?

LIZ. Not yet. Writer's block.

MYRON. Gabe doesn't get killed in the accident, but is paralyzed and Claire's love gives him the strength to walk again.

LIZ. Oh, you're good.

MYRON. Or Gabe does get killed in the car wreck, but / we find out that –

LIZ. I don't think Gabe should get killed. That's what I have to change. He can't die. The reader has certain expectations.

MYRON. Well, without the car accident the story seems pretty, I don't know...boring.

LIZ. Myron!

MYRON. Who wants to read about a guy and a girl who get married, have a kid, and have the perfect life?

LIZ. I do. Lots of people do.

(*Quiet.*)

MYRON. Do you want kids?

LIZ. What?

MYRON. I'm just curious! Not in a "let's have kids" way, but just in general, do you want kids or is your career too… or like…is it a thing for you?

LIZ. Um.

MYRON. Sorry. Is that weird to ask?

LIZ. Do you? Do you want kids?

MYRON. Maybe. I'm still pretty young, my career isn't where I want it to be. But yeah. One day. Yeah.

LIZ. Right.

MYRON. Liz, I think you have a Chick Lit hit on your hands.

LIZ. Romance, I write romance!

MYRON. Chick Lit!

LIZ. I'll think of a happy ending.

MYRON. Boring.

LIZ. I did not know I was on a first date with a fiction genre expert. Here I was, thinking you were just a trumpet player in the pit orchestra of *Wicked*.

MYRON. Okay, I am a jazz musician who must make a living.

LIZ. You know, in romance novels, certain occupations of heroes have proven to negatively affect sales: actor, dancer, sculptor, painter –

MYRON. Jazz musician who pays the bills by playing in the pit orchestra of *Wicked*.

LIZ. Hate to break it to you. And also…your name.

MYRON. What's wrong with my name?

LIZ. Alpha heroes have to be named something like Rafe, Cord, Kyle, or Rick –

MYRON. Rafe?

LIZ. It's a strong name.

MYRON. Rafe is a dumb name. Cord?

LIZ. It's a hard sound that indicates masculinity: CORD.

MYRON. My dreams are shattered.

LIZ. Myron: The Sad Jazz Trumpet Player.

MYRON. Liz: The Lonely Romance Novelist.

> *(They laugh. Beat.)*

I've gone on a couple of these internet date things and I don't know, it never feels…easy.

LIZ. Oh?

MYRON. But, this is easy. I feel like this is really fun and easy!

LIZ. I feel like this is really fun and easy, too!

MYRON. Do you really think I'm Myron, The Sad Jazz Trumpet Player?

LIZ. Do you really think I'm Liz, The Lonely Romance Novelist?

MYRON. No.

Scene Nine

(LIZ packs LILY's lunch. LILY rides out of her room on a scooter.)

LILY. On Saturday I will be seven!

LIZ. That's right, Miss Almost Birthday Girl! Where is your helmet? We're gonna be late for school.

> *(LILY rides around the apartment on her scooter, while LIZ searches for the helmet.)*

LILY. When Me and Silly play – pretend grown-ups, I'm a Rockette like Penny from *Dirty Dancing*. We share a huge loft apartment and you and Enshantay live there too! And we put on shows for lots of people in our loft apartment. And we have a girl dog and her and Spaghetti have puppies.

LIZ. What about your husband? Does he live in the loft apartment with all of us?

LILY. No. I don't have a husband when I am a grown-up. I have lots of boyfriends, though.

LIZ. What? *(Finding the helmet.)* Here it is.

LILY. All of our boyfriends come to our loft apartment, but we don't have husbands.

LIZ. Lily, come here and put on your helmet.

LILY. No! Silly said that it's dumb that kids have to wear helmets when they ride scooters.

LIZ. She shouldn't have said that.

LILY. Is Spaghetti gonna die?

LIZ. Oh, baby. He's just at the vet getting his tummy fixed.

LILY. I hope he dies. Daddy loves Spaghetti and if Spaghetti is dead then that means he's in Heaven with Daddy.

LIZ. Come here, please. Helmet.

LILY. No! Heaven is, like, the best place ever. Better than a Disney cruise, I bet.

LIZ. Sounds fun.

LILY. Not to Silly. She said that Heaven was a sham. Then she gave me the book.

LIZ. What book?

LILY. *Whispering Willow: A Story for Children About Dying.*

LIZ. I didn't know she gave you that book. Why haven't you shown it to me?

LILY. Silly told me not to. Ooh, also, Silly says that when we are grown-ups you're gonna be a writer! Do you want to be a writer like I want to be a Rockette?

LIZ. No, I don't want to be a writer. I am a…mother. Come here and put your helmet on.

LILY. NO.

(**LIZ** *puts the helmet on* **LILY**.)

LIZ. You need to wear a helmet.

LILY. This helmet sucks dick!

LIZ. What did you just say?

LILY. …

LIZ. Lillian Hollis Eberwine, where did you hear that?

LILY. I don't know.

LIZ. Lily, that is something that you are never allowed to say again. Do you understand?

LILY. Why?

LIZ. Because those are bad words. Lily, please tell me where you heard that.

LILY. I don't know.

LIZ. If you tell me where you heard it, I will tell you what it means.

LILY. The other night while you were out, I heard Enshantay tell Silly that our apartment's Wi-Fi sucks dick.

LIZ. Oh my God.

LILY. What does it mean?

LIZ. You can't say that anymore, Lily.

LILY. You said you would tell me what it means when something sucks dick!

LIZ. Okay. It's a bad saying. You know what a saying is? It's like, "Don't cry over spilt milk." Something that people just sort of say.

LILY. Like, "Girl, you better work"?

LIZ. Umm, yes. But there are some sayings that aren't nice.

LILY. Why do Enshantay and Silly say them if they're not nice?

LIZ. They just, sometimes they just slip. Bad words, sayings, can just slip. Okay? Now put this helmet on because we gotta get to school and hand out invitations to…

(*LILY lets LIZ put her helmet on.*)

LILY. My birthday party!

LIZ. The best Disney Princess birthday party ever! Now, let's scoot.

(*LILY yells toward BERNIE's room.*)

LILY. Bye, Silly!

(*BERNIE yells back, half-asleep. She sounds rough.*)

BERNIE. (*Offstage.*) Bye, Dill. Have school good day. Love you.

LILY. I love you as big as the sky!

(*As LILY and LIZ exit:*)

So, that's a saying too, huh? "I love you as big as the sky"?

LIZ. Yes. A good one. That's a good one.

Scene Ten

*(**LIZ** and **MYRON** on a park bench.)*

LIZ. The story is focused on character growth, but in romance novels character growth means that the hero and heroine grow towards, and for, one another. So, Gabe doesn't die.

MYRON. He's gotta die!

LIZ. I told you, happy ending.

MYRON. After he dies, maybe she like finds herself and some strong, like independent woman stuff starts happening.

LIZ. Ugh, I hate the "Single Woman's Quest."

MYRON. What?

LIZ. "She finds that what she needed from a man, she found in herself." I hate it. Men get the "Hero's Journey," with no expectation about whether or not romance is involved, but women get the "Single Woman's Quest." That's the most empowering story we get: one that is always contingent on a woman's relationship or lack thereof. It's deceptively sexist.

MYRON. You don't think romance novels are sexist? They encourage the belief that happily ever after only happens when a heroine finds love.

LIZ. …

MYRON. You think that? You think that!

LIZ. I don't think everything is fine and dandy if you don't have that.

MYRON. You just said that for men, the hero's journey is not dependent on love so I'm / confused –

LIZ. I don't necessarily like the rules, Myron. But I don't pretend they don't exist.

MYRON. The rules? Don't you think following rules based on gender is a little naive?

LIZ. I am the least naive person you will ever meet. You have no idea what my life experience has been.

MYRON. I don't pretend to. I'm sorry. So, tell me. About your life experience. I want to know who you are.

LIZ. You are such a musician.

MYRON. I do! I wanna know you.

LIZ. Well, I wanna know you, too.

MYRON. Okay.

LIZ. Okay, what?

MYRON. Let's know each other.

> *(Beat.)*

LIZ. Um…so. Go. Go ahead.

MYRON. I have to go first?

LIZ. It's your idea!

MYRON. Getting to know someone is not anyone's, like, original idea!

> *(They laugh.)*

What do you want to know?

LIZ. I guess…relationship stuff? Your last relationship. I guess.

MYRON. So that you can use it as fodder for your next novel?

LIZ. I am sure your love life is prime material for a romance novel.

MYRON. You're mean!

LIZ. I'm kidding. Go ahead.

MYRON. Um. I've never…

LIZ. Been in a relationship?

MYRON. No, no. I've never really talked about…I don't talk about my relationship stuff much, I guess. Ever. Really.

LIZ. You don't have to.

MYRON. No. No. Let's do this. Okay. So.

> *(**MYRON** looks at **LIZ**. A beat. Then, he goes for it.)*

I was with a woman for three years. Her name was Stephanie. She was a musical theatre actress. She had the Chinese symbol for "Dream" tattooed on her ankle.

LIZ. Ha!

MYRON. She didn't believe in tipping at restaurants. She was really into dolphins.

LIZ. Oh dear.

MYRON. I don't know what I was thinking. I just was…I was in love. I guess I was thinking, "I'm in love." I was all in, you know?

LIZ. I do.

MYRON. I thought I was so lucky. But really, I was just so stupid.

LIZ. You're not stupid for having been in love with someone.

MYRON. She was cheating on me. The entire time.

LIZ. Oh, no.

MYRON. I found these texts.

LIZ. She was texting someone romantic messages?

MYRON. Well, they weren't romantic. And they were pictures.

LIZ. What were they pictures of?

MYRON. She texted this guy pictures of her fingering herself.

LIZ. Oh my God.

MYRON. It was this guy I knew, so that made it even / worse.

LIZ. People do that?!

MYRON. Have affairs? Yes, they do.

LIZ. No, take pictures like that?!

MYRON. Pictures of them fingering / themselves –

LIZ. Please stop saying that!

MYRON. What, you've never sent –

LIZ. No!

MYRON. Not even, like, boobs?

LIZ. NO!

MYRON. Don't take this the wrong way.

LIZ. Don't say the wrong thing.

MYRON. You're cute.

> (**LIZ** *gets up and starts walking away.* **MYRON** *runs after her and grabs her hand.*)

Sorry, I didn't mean…I'm just. You're…it's really nice.

LIZ. I'm sorry about Stephanie.

MYRON. Yeah.

LIZ. Maybe she was confused, maybe she was going through a hard time –

MYRON. No. She cheated because she's a cheater. And she lied because she's a liar.

> (*Beat.*)

LIZ. Scared you, huh?

MYRON. Yeah.

LIZ. And do you still feel that way? Scared?

MYRON. I don't know. I might be coming around.

> (*Beat.*)

LIZ. Myron. I have to tell you something.

MYRON. Oh. Okay.

> (**LIZ** *pulls up her sleeve to reveal a tattoo of a Chinese symbol.*)

Oh no! No!

LIZ. I know! It's the worst! My sister and I got matching ones when I was like, fifteen.

MYRON. What does it mean? Oh God.

LIZ. It's the symbol for "sisters." It's horrible. But don't worry, I hate dolphins.

MYRON. Thank God.

LIZ. Every year I take a trip to Japan and I just kill a bunch of dolphins.

> (*They laugh.*)

MYRON. I smile a lot when I'm with you.

LIZ. I smile a lot when I'm with you.

MYRON. Copycat.

LIZ. Copycat.

MYRON. Oh, that's what we're doing?

LIZ. Oh, that's what we're doing?

MYRON. Okay, then.

LIZ. Okay, then.

MYRON. Kiss me.

LIZ. Kiss me.

>*(**MYRON** goes to kiss **LIZ**. **LIZ** stops him.)*

Wait!

MYRON. You just said "kiss / me."

LIZ. The game, I thought we were playing that game, I didn't really –

MYRON. Oh.

LIZ. Sorry.

>*(Beat.)*

MYRON. I would like to kiss you.

>*(**LIZ** looks at him. They stare at each other for a bit.*
>*__LIZ__ offers her hand to **MYRON**. He laughs a little,*
>*then kisses it.)*

>*(Beat.)*

Okay, so Gabe dies and then Claire travels to Italy, India, Bali –

LIZ. Myron.

MYRON. What?

LIZ. It's my story.

MYRON. Fine. He doesn't die.

LIZ. That's right. Happy ending.

Scene Eleven

(**LILY** *reads from the laptop.*)

LILY. What is the secret to true love? A. Faith. B. Compassion.

BERNIE. C. There is no such thing as true love. Is that an option on the "Which Disney Princess Are You?" quiz?

(**LIZ** *enters.*)

LILY. No!

BERNIE. This quiz is stupid.

LIZ. The Disney Princess Quiz? It's not stupid! I thought it would be fun for y'all to do while I was…at my meeting. My parent meeting.

BERNIE. How was your meeting, Liz? In the park? Was it productive?

LIZ. Yes. Yep. Yepyepyep.

(**LIZ** *sits with* **LILY** *and reads from the screen.*)

Okay. For you, "Happily Ever After" is: A. In a –

BERNIE. You know what's even better than "Happily Ever After"? The very beginning. The "I can't stop thinking about you every second" part. There is an actual term for this, it's called limerence. But once things fall into place, the limerence disappears.

LIZ. "Happily Ever After" is –

BERNIE. I say, sober up from being drunk off of one person, move on to the next. After the beginning, things just always get sad.

LIZ. Things don't always get sad.

BERNIE. Liz. You of all people should know that things always get sad.

LIZ. "Happily Ever After" is: A. In a caring relationship. B. In a castle.

BERNIE. No more quiz, y'all.

LIZ. We have to figure out which princess you are for Lily's party.

BERNIE. I'm the one who likes anal.

LIZ. Bernie! Dill. I...me and Silly need to talk about some surprise birthday stuff. Can you go play in your room for a minute?

LILY. What surprise birthday stuff?

LIZ. Well, now if we told you it wouldn't be a surprise, now would it?

BERNIE. Duh!

LIZ. Go on, baby.

> (**LILY** *runs to her room.*)

Bernie. You can't say those things in front of Lily. I gave y'all that quiz to do –

BERNIE. So that you could go get freak nasty with Myron in the park!

LIZ. Because I didn't want y'all watching R-rated movies / or –

BERNIE. Give me the deetz. Was there any up the shirt down the pants?

LIZ. Bernie, I'm serious, you –

BERNIE. You're always real tight-lipped about Myron. Makes me nervous that you actually like this little nerd.

LIZ. Myron is a great guy, and –

BERNIE. That's good. But keep it easy. Keep it fun. We don't want another Bradley situation.

LIZ. Excuse me?

BERNIE. This is your time to look around and really discover what it is that you want.

LIZ. I want my life back. My life with my family was everything that I ever wanted.

BERNIE. To be stuck in that little town with one man and a kid was everything that you ever wanted?

LIZ. Yes!

BERNIE. Liz.

LIZ. What?

BERNIE. That's retarded.

LIZ. That word, Bernie!

BERNIE. You're brainwashed by the standard narrative –

LIZ. No, I'm not. I'm not like you.

BERNIE. And the life that you always "dreamed of" was a life that was instilled by a patriarchal society.

LIZ. You sound like an angsty teenager. You think it's black or white.

BERNIE. Girl, you know I don't think it's black or white.

> (**BERNIE** *picks her nose and wipes it on the back of the couch.*)

LIZ. Bernie!

BERNIE. What?

LIZ. You just picked your nose and wiped it on the back of the couch!

BERNIE. So?

LIZ. So, that's disgusting!

BERNIE. Loosen up.

LIZ. Lily has been doing that and that is because she has seen you do it!

BERNIE. I do it because Lily does it!

LIZ. Jesus, Bernie. Grow up.

BERNIE. I'm sorry, what?

LIZ. You just wiped a booger on the back of the couch. Grow up.

BERNIE. Girl, you have got to get laid. We gotta knock something loose up in there.

LIZ. BERNIE, SHUT UP! Shut up about me getting laid and things ending sad and me wanting things I don't want and saying my Wi-Fi sucks dick.

BERNIE. What?

LIZ. Yeah! Lily told me she heard you and Enshantay saying that our Wi-Fi sucks dick.

BERNIE. Your Wi-Fi does suck dick. You need a new router. And Enshantay is the one that said it.

LIZ. See, even that! You don't take responsibility for anything.

BERNIE. I take responsibility.

LIZ. For what?!

BERNIE. Where is this coming from?

LIZ. You act like you're this grown-up, progressive woman but you don't know shit.

BERNIE. Are we really having this conversation? All because I wiped a fucking booger / on the couch?

LIZ. It's not just the booger! It's everything! You say you want to be a parent to Lily? Well, you're doing everything wrong! She sees you as a role model.

BERNIE. You don't think I'm a good role model for Lily?!

LIZ. I don't want her to think that there's no such thing as true love and that she shouldn't get married and that it's okay to say things that are filthy.

BERNIE. Oh my God, Liz. You are so fucking backwards.

LIZ. I'm not backwards. I have a six-year-old and I am trying to raise her properly. She can't say her scooter helmet sucks dick!

> (**BERNIE** *starts laughing.*)

It's not funny! And no more death talk. No more sneaking her Weeping Willow death books and telling her to hide them from me.

BERNIE. It's called, *Whispering Willow: A Story for Children About Dying* and I think it's a good way to teach her / about death.

LIZ. I don't want to teach her about death. I will teach her about death when she is old enough to handle it.

BERNIE. I was her age when Mom died, you were four and it was damn hard, but we handled it.

LIZ. We handled it? Is that right? Then how come you are terrified of a lasting relationship? Of anything serious?!

BERNIE. Are you like, trying to be my therapist or some shit? My life choices have nothing to do with Mom dying.

LIZ. They're not life choices! They're survival skills!

BERNIE. What about jumping into something with someone after a couple of dates?

LIZ. I'm not jumping into anything!

BERNIE. Right after your husband dies? What's that called?

LIZ. I like Myron! He makes me smile! And you were the one who told me that I should –

BERNIE. Get laid. I told you that you needed to start fucking.

LIZ. Stop! Stop talking like that!

BERNIE. Sorry. Here in survivor land, we say "FUCKING" because that's all that it really is!

LIZ. What happened to you? How on Earth did you get this way?

BERNIE. I didn't have a knight in shining armor swoop in and rescue me from reality. That's what happened to me. My life didn't turn into a fucking fairy tale. My question is this: how can you be a mother when, Liz; you're still a little girl? You are the one who never grew up.

LIZ. If growing up means turning into you, then I want nothing to do with it.

BERNIE. Go fuck yourself.

> (**BERNIE** *grabs her purse.*)

With a big, gigantic dildo. Do you know what a dildo is, Liz?

LIZ. Yes, I know what a dildo is!

BERNIE. Oh yeah? What is it?

LIZ. It's…a…a dildo is a fake penis!

> (**BERNIE** *gives* **LIZ** *a shitty "thumbs up" sign and begins grabbing her things.*)

Where are you going?

BERNIE. I'm gonna go fuck this carpenter slash karaoke host that I just met at Rite Aid. I think his name is Mike. Then, I'm gonna buy a pack of cigarettes from the deli. Then, I'm gonna sit in Enshantay's tub and smoke. And I'm not gonna crack a window. And I'm gonna feel fucking great about it.

> (**BERNIE** *leaves and slams the door.* **LIZ** *takes a look around her empty apartment.*)

LIZ. Oh dear.

Scene Twelve

(The next day. **MYRON** *is nervously prepping his apartment. The buzzer rings, and he opens the door to* **LIZ**. *She holds several shopping bags.)*

MYRON. Hi!

LIZ. Are you okay?

MYRON. What?

LIZ. You asked me to come over right away, are you okay?

MYRON. Yeah, yeah. Here, come in.

LIZ. Is everything alright?

MYRON. Yeah. Yes. You've been shopping?

LIZ. Yeah, um. Running errands.

MYRON. You're not writing today?

LIZ. Day off. Why did you want me to come over?

MYRON. I woke up thinking about this riff. I can't figure out how it ends. I thought that you could help me. Like, how we talk about the ending / of your book.

LIZ. You called me over here so that we could talk about how your trumpet riff will end?

MYRON. Is that okay?

LIZ. Yeah. Yes.

MYRON. Great. Great. So, come in, come in.

(He fully opens the door, and they enter his apartment. It is a musician's apartment.)

LIZ. This is nice.

MYRON. Yeah? The original Murphy bed always makes the panties drop.

LIZ. What?!

MYRON. What?! I'm just kidding! I'm kidding! But this is an original Murphy bed. So. Here, put your stuff down. I'll pour us some coffee. I went out and got you some almond milk.

LIZ. Oh, that's so sweet!

MYRON. Uh-oh, I know how you take your coffee. You know what that means!

LIZ. What?

MYRON. Uh, just. I got…here we go with…the almond milk…yeah. Here you go.

> (*He brings over coffee. The two sit on the Murphy bed.*)

LIZ. So, the riff?

MYRON. Right! Right.

> (**MYRON** *picks up his trumpet.*)

I'm nervous.

LIZ. No! Don't be nervous. I'll love it. I know I will.

MYRON. Okay. Um, yeah. Okay. Here goes.

> (*Another small pause.*)

I had a great time with you, the other day.

LIZ. I did, too.

MYRON. It was, like, a truly lovely afternoon.

LIZ. It was. It was really lovely.

> (*Pause.*)

You don't know how to play the trumpet, do you?

MYRON. No clue.

LIZ. I knew it!

MYRON. Is that what this thing is?!

LIZ. Oh, the deception!

> (*They laugh. Beat.*)

Please.

> (**MYRON** *begins to play.* * *The riff starts off too loudly, with a few missed notes. As* **MYRON** *gets more comfortable, the music begins to find its flow and it is lovely, sweet.* **LIZ** *closes her eyes to listen.*

---

*The publisher and author suggest that the licensee create an original composition for this section.

Then, the sound stops abruptly, and **MYRON** *and*
LIZ *sit in silence for a moment.)*

MYRON. That's it. I don't know how it ends.

LIZ. It's really…wow. I don't know why you think you
needed me. It's really / wonderful.

MYRON. I needed you to come over because I needed to
see you.

LIZ. Oh.

MYRON. I needed to kiss you.

LIZ. Oh.

MYRON. I like you. I really like you.

LIZ. I really like you, too.

MYRON. I wanna know you.

LIZ. We know each other, remember?

MYRON. No. We don't. Can I kiss you?

> *(Beat.)*

LIZ. Yes.

> *(He kisses her. She kisses him right back.)*

When writing love scenes in romance novels, setting is
crucial.

MYRON. Oh yeah?

> *(They kiss again.)*

LIZ. You either need a big bed, satin sheets…

MYRON. Candles, rose petals everywhere?

> *(**MYRON** begins kissing **LIZ**'s neck, her ear.)*

LIZ. Or, um, a construction site: where a wooden palette
serves as a bed and dirt flies.

MYRON. There's no rule about a musician's old Brooklyn
apartment at 11:13 a.m. on a Saturday?

LIZ. Not yet.

> *(**LIZ** kisses **MYRON** deeply. **MYRON** touches **LIZ**'s
> breast above her shirt. She gasps.)*

MYRON. Is that okay?

LIZ. Yep. Yep. Totally. One hundred percent okay. Totally fine and okay and great and fun. Your hand right there is fun. It is fun stuff.

> *(They kiss more.* **MYRON** *unbuttons* **LIZ***'s shirt.)*

MYRON. Liz. You are stunning.

LIZ. This is like, my worst bra. I think it's from the ninth grade. I didn't think anyone would see it. So. It used to be baby blue and now it just is kind of grey. And fuzz. There are these fuzz balls. See? But. Thank you. Thanks. I have some better bras at home. So.

> *(She kisses* **MYRON**. *We see something give.* **LIZ** *kisses, touches, moves with deep hunger. She begs, hopes: "Maybe this will work!" It's hot, gorgeous; but it is desperate.* **MYRON** *also gives over to something. Their make out turns into something authentic. Sexy. Scary.* **MYRON** *touches* **LIZ** *between her legs. It's good. It's great. And then, just in time,* **LIZ** *jumps up and begins buttoning her shirt.)*

Woo! I have to go. Umm…I have to go and write.

MYRON. I thought you weren't writing today.

LIZ. I just remembered this deadline, it just popped into my head.

MYRON. I thought this…what we were doing…felt good. I thought it was good.

LIZ. It is! It is good! *(Buttoning her shirt.)* Three rules about um, love scenes, sex scenes. One. Make 'em wait. Two. Let 'em start and then make 'em stop. Three. Leave 'em wanting more.

MYRON. I'm a little confused.

LIZ. Everything is fine. I just. I have to go.

> *(She leaves.* **MYRON** *sees the shopping bags. He grabs them and runs to the hallway.)*

MYRON. Liz! Wait!

> *(She's gone.)*

Shit. Shit.

Scene Thirteen

(**LIZ** *runs around the apartment trying to decorate for* **LILY**'s *birthday. There are napkins and plates of all sorts, a "Dirty Thirty" banner, Christmas decorations, a cardboard Halloween Witch.*)

LILY. *(Offstage.)* Can I come out now, Mama?

LIZ. You have to take a bath, Dill. Have you taken a bath?

LILY. *(Offstage.)* Yes?

LIZ. I didn't hear any water running. Take a bath, get dressed, and then you can come in here.

LILY. *(Offstage.)* But I don't have my / Jasmine costume.

LIZ. Bath! Now, please.

(**BERNIE** *walks in with presents and is dressed up as Belle from* Beauty and the Beast. *She is not messing around. She has hair extensions.*)

Whoa! Wow!

BERNIE. I am vehemently opposed to the Disney Princess franchise, but if this is what Lily wanted for her birthday party, then I must go whole hog. I finished the quiz and it turns out, that I am Belle. From *Beauty and the Beast.*

LIZ. It looks good in here, right? Festive?

BERNIE. It looks like a straight-up dumpster fire. What is going on with this decor?

LIZ. I am freaking out. I left my bags with all the Disney Princess decorations at Myron's.

BERNIE. You got an Entenmann's cake?!

LIZ. I left her cake, too! There wasn't time to get anything else. I was getting my freak on and now, because of that, my daughter is gonna have a shitty birthday party. I'm the worst mom in the whole f'ing world.

(Beat. **LIZ** *continues to try and decorate.)*

You stay at Enshantay's last night? Oooh, or at that karaoke Rite Aid cashier's?

BERNIE. ...

LIZ. Girl.

BERNIE. What girl?

LIZ. You're still mad? About yesterday? Really?

BERNIE. I told Enshantay that it was best if she didn't come.

LIZ. Why did you do that?

BERNIE. Oh, we have to set a certain example for Lily. We wouldn't want an insanely kind and hilarious drag queen in an extravagant Snow White costume around these impressionable young children. That wouldn't be fun for anyone.

LIZ. Bernie.

BERNIE. Where's Lily?

LIZ. In the tub. I left her costume at Myron's –

BERNIE. It is a THEME party.

LIZ. Yeah, I know! Because I was slutting it out my daughter doesn't have a costume for her own birthday party. I'm a horrible mom and a horrible sister. I get it, okay? Lily's friends and their parents will be here soon, and / I –

BERNIE. Hey birthday girl?! I'm gonna help you get dressed!

LILY. *(Offstage.)* I have a Jasmine costume!

BERNIE. No Princess Jasmine! We're gonna create a new character! You can be anything! You can wear whatever your heart desires!

> *(**BERNIE** goes to **LILY**'s room. **LIZ** takes a deep breath. The doorbell rings.)*

LIZ. No one likes the person who comes early to the party.

> *(She opens the door to **CEECEE** and **PAPA BOBBY** **EBERWINE**: Fifties, well-dressed, holding suitcases, and loaded with presents.)*

CEECEE & PAPA BOBBY. Surprise!

LIZ. CeeCee?! Papa Bobby?!

CEECEE. Here we are!

LIZ. What…what in the world?

CEECEE. We came to surprise the birthday girl!

PAPA BOBBY. I told ol' girl we should let you know.

CEECEE. But I knew you were preparing for the party.

PAPA BOBBY. She said she didn't want you to have to worry about your in-laws coming into town.

CEECEE. You know having to clean for us, entertain us –

PAPA BOBBY. But I said we should –

CEECEE. Well, look at you, Elizabeth.

PAPA BOBBY. You look great. You've been eating avocados?

LIZ. Uh…

PAPA BOBBY. Or some other type of healthy fat?

CEECEE. He's drunk, Liz

PAPA BOBBY. You okay, Elizabeth?

LIZ. Yes sir. I just. Hi. You're here.

CEECEE. Yes, we are!

LIZ. Come in. Come in.

CEECEE. So this is the place?

LIZ. Yes ma'am. Um, welcome.

CEECEE. It's so…funky.

PAPA BOBBY. Where's Spaghetti?

CEECEE. We flew right in, hailed a cab, and he brought us right here.

LIZ. Spaghetti's in the back garden.

CEECEE. Our little taxi driver was so interesting. He was from Pakistan.

PAPA BOBBY. Which way's the garden?

LIZ. Um, here, I'll show you –

(**CEECEE** *spots a picture.*)

CEECEE. I've never seen this. Liz, when did y'all take this picture?

LIZ. Oh, um, last year.

CEECEE. Where are y'all? / Seaside?

LIZ. Seaside. Yes ma'am.

CEECEE. Bobby, come look at this picture.

> *(They all look at the picture. Pause.)*

It's Bradley, Liz, and Lily at sunset. Look at my boy.

PAPA BOBBY. What a beautiful family. That sure is a nice picture.

CEECEE. Liz, let's get this blown up and framed. I would hate for someone to miss it. I have a wonderful framer in / Holly Grove.

LIZ. I can find a framer / here.

CEECEE. I can take it to my / little framer.

PAPA BOBBY. She can find a framer in New York, Cecilia.

CEECEE. Can you get him a drink, Liz? And I would love a glass of Sancerre.

LIZ. Yes ma'am. Um, sure.

> *(**LIZ** tries to find something to give them.)*

CEECEE. Can you believe we're here?

LIZ. No! No, ma'am!

PAPA BOBBY. Liz, I said we should have checked in with you.

CEECEE. But I said, "Family does not need to check in!"

PAPA BOBBY. Can Spaghetti come in? I really would like to see / that dog.

CEECEE. You said that once you got settled, we could come visit, and my goodness, it's been almost / a month!

PAPA BOBBY. Are you settled, Liz?

LIZ. Yes, yes sir. I'm…settled.

> *(**LIZ** hands them drinks and pours herself a large glass of wine, which she refills throughout this scene. **PAPA BOBBY** spots the book.)*

PAPA BOBBY. *Writing a Romance Novel for Dummies.*

CEECEE. You're writing romance novels these days, Liz?

LIZ. No ma'am. Bernie got that for me as a joke.

CEECEE. That's cute.

PAPA BOBBY. I think that's a great idea, Liz, you've always loved to read.

CEECEE. Liz is a full-time mother. That's a twenty-four hour, seven day a week career, Bobby.

PAPA BOBBY. I know, I just think / it's a good idea.

CEECEE. Men don't understand how being a full-time mother actually is FULL-TIME.

PAPA BOBBY. I do understand, Cecilia, but maybe Liz wants to do / other things.

CEECEE. He started drinking at ten, Liz.

PAPA BOBBY. So did you, ol' girl.

CEECEE. He said that if you are not drinking in first class that's just like spitting in the faces of all those people who have to sit in coach.

PAPA BOBBY. You said that, Cecilia.

LIZ. Could y'all help me get this stuff together? People should be here / soon.

CEECEE. What's the theme?

LIZ. Oh. Um…the theme is…birthday party.

CEECEE. A child's birthday party has to have a theme, Liz. You and Bradley always had the greatest themes for Lily's birthday parties. Y'all did Dr. Seuss that one year and Bradley dressed up as The Cat in the Hat.

PAPA BOBBY. Then there was the Smurf party where we all painted ourselves blue.

CEECEE. Bradley made us! He insisted!

LIZ. I had decorations for a Disney Princess theme. But I got mugged.

CEECEE. Oh my God.

LIZ. This afternoon. I got mugged. I didn't have time to go back to the party store, so I just tried to make do.

PAPA BOBBY. You were mugged?

CEECEE. Liz, you were mugged at gunpoint.

LIZ. No! Easy. Easy mugging. He just grabbed the bags. Grabbed the bags with the birthday stuff and ran. Um, quick, could you hang these?

(She throws **CEECEE** *a single roll of streamers.)*

CEECEE. These streamers have "Save The Ta-Tas" printed all over them.

LIZ. Bernie had a fundraiser, she thought she was gonna run a marathon for breast cancer.

CEECEE. Elizabeth, does Bernice have breast cancer?

LIZ. Just an awareness marathon, she knows somebody –

PAPA BOBBY. You can support breast cancer awareness without actually having breast cancer / Cecilia.

CEECEE. I know that. Liz, I'm sure you don't miss hanging around with this genius.

PAPA BOBBY. I'm gonna go see Spaghetti.

CEECEE. You're gonna help me with these breast cancer awareness streamers is what you're / gonna do.

BERNIE. *(Offstage.)* The one and only Lily Dilly Hollis Eberwine! Serving some serious independent woman realness!

> *(***LILY*** *walks in wearing a magician's hat, a pink wig, a coconut bra over a golden leotard, a mermaid skirt, and ballet shoes. She is holding a magic wand and a sword.)*

LILY. CeeCee! Papa Bobby!

CEECEE. My Dilly!

PAPA BOBBY. Surprise!

BERNIE. *(To the* **EBERWINES**.*)* Wow. What are y'all doing here?

PAPA BOBBY. Hey there, Bernie! We flew up this morning to surprise our Dill!

LIZ. Wow! Dill, I love your costume!

CEECEE. Elizabeth, Lily is wearing a coconut bra.

BERNIE. Yes, girl!

LIZ. Oh, sorry. Dill, I'm gonna grab your blue cardigan, to wear / over –

LILY. No! I don't want to wear the blue cardigan.

LIZ. We just need to put a little something over –

LILY. That blue cardigan sucks dick!

    (Beat.)

BERNIE. I told her she had to stop saying that, y'all.

LILY. It slipped!

BERNIE. Don't be mad, it's her birthday!

LIZ. Lily, if I hear that one more time –

CEECEE. This is something she has said more / than once?

LIZ. She heard it somewhere. I think. Um, a violent video game.

CEECEE. She plays violent video games?

LIZ. At a friend's house. A friend who comes from a broken home. No more! You understand?

LILY. Yes!

CEECEE. Yes ma'am. Now, Dill, you go ahead and open this before everyone gets here. It's a special something.

    *(The doorbell rings. **LIZ** opens the door to reveal **MYRON** with bags full of Disney Princess party supplies.)*

LIZ. Hi.

MYRON. Hello.

LIZ. How did you find my apartment?

MYRON. Your wallet was in this bag. I thought since it was a birthday it was pretty important. There's a cake.

    *(**LILY** has ripped open the package and is holding a baseball mitt.)*

LILY. Mama!

    *(**LIZ** does not look at **LILY**.)*

    Mama, look!

MYRON. Liz?

LILY. Mama! Mama! Look, Mama! Mama!

MYRON. Liz, I think she's talking to you.

LIZ. Yes.

LILY. LOOK!

LIZ. *(Looking.)* I see, baby.

PAPA BOBBY. That was your daddy's. It's pretty worn out, but he loved it. Wouldn't get a new one.

CEECEE. Your daddy and Papa Bobby would play catch in our front yard for hours and hours. Remember that, Liz? We could never figure out how the two of them just stood there, throwing that ball, not saying a word.

PAPA BOBBY. Quiet can be real nice, Cecilia.

LILY. Mama, who's that?

MYRON. Hey there. I'm / Myron.

LIZ. Myron! Everybody! This. Is. MYRON!

BERNIE. Shit. On. Tits.

LIZ. Bernie!

CEECEE. Hello, Myron. Is your child a friend of our Lily?

LIZ. Myron, he, um, saw me getting mugged earlier today.

BERNIE. Girl, you got mugged?!

LIZ. Easy mugging. The guy just took my bags and ran and Myron saw the whole thing. He chased the guy down, got my bags back, found my address and came here! How about that for the kindness of strangers?

PAPA BOBBY. Myron, let me shake your hand.

CEECEE. My goodness, this is unbelievable.

PAPA BOBBY. Pleasure to meet you. You're a fine man.

CEECEE. You chased the mugger down, Myron? What in the world did you do after you caught him?

LIZ. The mugger actually just handed over the bags, so it was no big deal. Myron just told me that. Here at the door. So, yay! We have Disney Princess supplies!

PAPA BOBBY. Can I get you a drink?

CEECEE. My goodness, you must be a wreck after such an ordeal.

PAPA BOBBY. What'll it be, Myron? You seem like a bourbon man.

LIZ. I'm sure Myron has to be / somewhere.

CEECEE. We're celebrating my granddaughter's seventh birthday. This is Lily, the birthday girl! You saved her party!

PAPA BOBBY. Here Myron. I made it a double.

MYRON. …Thanks

PAPA BOBBY. Cheers to Myron.

CEECEE. Young man, they do not make 'em like you anymore.

MYRON. Uh, Happy Birthday Lily.

LILY. Thanks!

MYRON. Liz, these are your parents?

CEECEE. We are her in-laws. But, that term doesn't really fit.

PAPA BOBBY. It certainly feels like Liz is our daughter.

LIZ. Bradley's…they're Bradley's…

(**LIZ** *drunkenly stumbles and falls.*)

LILY. Mama!

PAPA BOBBY. Whoopsy-daisy!

CEECEE. Elizabeth! Are you okay?

BERNIE. *(Catching* **LIZ***.)* Girl, why don't you just sit down. It's probably just all catching up with you. Even easy muggings can be traumatic. Here we go. Myron, you said there's a cake in one / of the bags?

MYRON. Yeah. Sorry. Here.

BERNIE. Thank you. Dill, why don't you show Papa Bobby and CeeCee the back garden? Y'all can see Spaghetti, but just a heads-up, he wears diapers now.

CEECEE. Spaghetti wears a diaper?

BERNIE. Yep. He's been dirty diarrheaing all over Brooklyn –

CEECEE. Let's not talk like that, please ma'am.

LIZ. Sorry.

CEECEE. You don't need to apologize, Elizabeth. Bernice knows we don't like potty talk.

PAPA BOBBY. Let's see this garden. I'm curious about the diaper.

> (**LILY** *gives* **LIZ** *the mitt and begins pulling* **PAPA BOBBY** *and* **CEECEE** *to the back door.*)

Dill, after your party we can play some catch. Sound good?

LILY. Yes!

CEECEE. Yes, sir.

LILY. Yes, sir.

> (*They are gone.* **BERNIE** *goes to the fridge.*)

MYRON. Liz?

> (**LIZ** *stares at the baseball glove. She doesn't move. She doesn't speak. She's drunk.*)

Please say something.

LIZ. …

MYRON. Okay. Wow. Okay.

> (**MYRON** *walks out.* **BERNIE** *follows him.*)

BERNIE. *(To* **LIZ**, *as she exits out the front door.)* What the fuck is going on, girl?

CEECEE. *(Offstage.)* Elizabeth you have left a very nice vase out here. I'm worried it's going to get ruined.

PAPA BOBBY. *(Offstage.)* That's a bong, Cecilia.

LILY. *(Offstage.)* That's Silly's!

CEECEE. *(Offstage.)* A bong?

PAPA BOBBY. *(Offstage.)* Yes. A bong. A bong for drugs.

Scene Fourteen

(**LIZ** *is asleep on the couch.* **BERNIE** *is washing dishes.* **LIZ** *wakes up, incredibly hungover.*)

LIZ. Bernie, where's Dill?

BERNIE. CeeCee and Papa Bobby decided to get a hotel. Lily went with them.

LIZ. What about…the party?

BERNIE. After you passed out on top of the Entenmann's cake, we thought it was best to cancel.

LIZ. Oh my God.

BERNIE. Papa Bobby and CeeCee made sure the hotel had a pool and Lily was excited about that. I put a sign on the door that said we had a sudden bed bug infestation, so we had to cancel the Disney Princess birthday party. Bases were covered.

LIZ. Thank you.

BERNIE. I was able to chase Myron down after he left yesterday. We had a little chat.

LIZ. Bernie, I feel terrible.

BERNIE. You told him you were a romance novelist.

LIZ. Please don't right now.

BERNIE. And…Liz. Liz, he had no idea you had a daughter. He didn't know about / Lily.

LIZ. He didn't need to know.

BERNIE. You tell me that me wiping a booger on the back of your couch is gonna fuck Lily up. You think this is being a good parent?

LIZ. Don't tell me I'm not a good parent. You don't know what this is like.

BERNIE. No, I don't. But I do know that you are dealing with it in a really retarded way.

LIZ. THAT WORD!

BERNIE. Oh, shut the fuck up. YOU LIED ABOUT LILY.

(*Pause.*)

BERNIE. You make me feel like shit for who I am.

LIZ. What?

BERNIE. You make me feel like shit.

LIZ. I never meant –

BERNIE. I know, girl. But you do. When you met Bradley, you left me.

LIZ. I didn't leave you.

BERNIE. I raised you, Liz. I took care of you. And you left me the moment some guy came along.

LIZ. Some guy? Bradley is some guy?

BERNIE. You got married and had your perfect life and you looked down on me.

LIZ. I admired you!

BERNIE. You judge me and tell me I'm a bad influence on your daughter. Who I love. Who I love more than anything.

LIZ. I know.

BERNIE. And I love you. More than anything.

LIZ. I love you so much.

BERNIE. It was great to reconnect with you in this way / in New York.

LIZ. It is great and I'm sorry / for yesterday.

BERNIE. But, there's a reason I left home and you stayed. We're different. And, at the end of the day, this just isn't gonna work. I think it's best if I move out.

LIZ. You can't move out. You can't leave us.

BERNIE. It's too confusing for Lily, the two of us teaching her different things.

LIZ. You can't leave, Lily loves you.

BERNIE. Me and Lily are gonna be best friends forever.

LIZ. Let's figure this out.

BERNIE. I think me leaving is the grown-up thing to do.

LIZ. This is working, we just need to iron out the kinks.

BERNIE. It's fake working. It's not fair to Dill.

(Beat.)

LIZ. I should have known. Typical. When something gets hard, you leave. We're past the beginning. No more limerence for me and Lily, huh Bernie?

BERNIE. Liz.

LIZ. The Lily and Liz adventure is over. Onto the next one.

BERNIE. You're one to talk. I'm a whole lot of fun until a man comes along. Isn't that right?

LIZ. Do you hate me because I got married and had a family?

BERNIE. Liz, I love you. I just. We are so different. We grew up to be so different.

LIZ. *(Quiet.)* You're...you're really leaving?

BERNIE. I am doing everything wrong. I'm not a good role model for Lily.

LIZ. I didn't mean that when / I said –

BERNIE. Yes, you did. And it's okay. But I'm not gonna change. The life I have has been hard-won. And I like it.

LIZ. I'm not asking you to change.

BERNIE. Okay. So, I'll stay and keep doing the things I do around Lily. Is that what you want?

(Beat.)

LIZ. No. No, that's not what I want.

BERNIE. Okay, then. CeeCee and Papa Bobby will be here later tonight. Maybe y'all can have a little birthday dinner, Lily's real cake is in the fridge –

LIZ. What am I supposed to do?! Tell me what I am supposed to do!

BERNIE. I don't know. But I think you're gonna figure it out. Because you are not a princess, girl. You're a superhero. I'll be back later this week to grab my shit. Why don't you jump in the shower before they get back. You sorta smell like a honky-tonk.

LIZ. I do?

BERNIE. You get a smell when you're real nervous, so there's that and then the booze...like a honky-tonk that serves fajitas.

LIZ. You always smell like that.

BERNIE. Well. At least now we have something in common.

    (**BERNIE** *leaves.*)

LIZ. Bernie.

Scene Fifteen

(**CEECEE**, **PAPA BOBBY**, **LIZ**, *and* **LILY** *eating takeout that evening.*)

LILY. This is soy protein, CeeCee.

CEECEE. Is that right?

LILY. Yes ma'am. And this is kale.

PAPA BOBBY. Which one of these has chicken?

LILY. This is from our vegetarian place!

PAPA BOBBY. They don't have chicken?

CEECEE. You would think that in at least one of these containers there would be chicken.

LIZ. I'm sorry there's no chicken.

CEECEE. Nobody asked you to apologize, sweetheart.

PAPA BOBBY. Do you still cook a lot, Liz?

LILY. She cooks every night! And everyone at school wants my lunch, because Mama packs the best lunches with all my favorite stuff and in every lunch she packs a note!

CEECEE. What do the notes say?

LILY. The same thing every day, "I love you as big as the sky."

(*Pause. They all know this saying from Bradley.*)

LIZ. The pool? At the hotel. Lily, was the pool at the hotel fun?

LILY. I dove!

CEECEE. In the shallow end, Liz. She could have killed herself.

LILY. My head could hit the bottom and then I / would die.

LIZ. Baby, you won't die if you dive in the –

CEECEE. – Shallow end of the pool? Yes, she most certainly will.

LILY. I would die and then I would be with Daddy!

LIZ. Lily.

LILY. I wanna die! I wanna die! I WANNA DIE!

LIZ. Lily, stop.

LILY. I wanna be dead with my daddy!

LIZ. Lily. SHUT UP. SHUT UP.

> *(Beat.)*

CEECEE. She can talk about her daddy, Elizabeth.

LIZ. You don't know what she can and can't talk about! I do! Because I am her mother!

> *(**LILY** starts crying.)*

CEECEE. Dill, it's okay, baby. Shhh, it's okay.

LIZ. No! No, it's not okay!

LILY. Why are you yelling at everybody?

LIZ. I don't know!

LILY. You're being so mean!

LIZ. I know!

> *(Pause.)*

PAPA BOBBY. Cecilia. Do something. Now. Please.

CEECEE. Okay, okay. Now everybody is just a little upset.

> *(**LIZ** tries to hold **LILY**. **LILY** shoves her away.)*

LIZ. Baby.

LILY. NO! NO! You're mean!

LIZ. I'm sorry, baby.

LILY. Don't touch me! I want my daddy! I want to go and be with my daddy!

CEECEE. Lily, baby.

LILY. I WANT TO BE DEAD. I WANNA DIE.

> *(**LILY** runs out. Beat.)*

LIZ. Y'all, I'm so sorry. I'll go talk to her –

CEECEE. I'll go. You stay right here. Just take a minute. Bobby, get her a drink.

LIZ. I'm so sorry.

CEECEE. You don't have to keep apologizing, sweetheart. Okay? I'll go. Lily and I can talk and play and I'll give her a hundred dollars. Pour more liquor in that glass, Bobby. Pretend you're making a drink for yourself.

*(A beat. LIZ sobs and **BOBBY** pours.)*

LIZ. I'm so sorry. I'm ashamed of myself.

PAPA BOBBY. Shhh. None of that.

LIZ. I'm so sorry.

PAPA BOBBY. Shhh.

LIZ. For the birthday party. For getting drunk.

PAPA BOBBY. Liz, I get drunk every single day.

(They laugh. Beat.)

LIZ. I don't know what I'm doing.

PAPA BOBBY. You're doing fine.

LIZ. I'm a bad mom.

PAPA BOBBY. I'm not having that kind of talk, Elizabeth Eberwine.

LIZ. I don't know how to do this.

(Pause.)

PAPA BOBBY. I don't either.

LIZ. We were strong, we did good, and now it's time for him to come back. I'm ready for him to come back. I want him to come back.

PAPA BOBBY. I do, too.

LIZ. I don't know what to do without him. I don't know how to raise her. I don't know how to set an example.

PAPA BOBBY. You're setting a great example. You're trying to move forward, to live a life –

LIZ. All I ever wanted was the life we had. I don't want another one. I don't want the Single Woman's Quest!

*(**LIZ** breaks down sobbing. Beat.)*

PAPA BOBBY. I don't know what that means.

LIZ. I can't do this.

PAPA BOBBY. Yes, you can. Let us help you, sweetie.

LIZ. You do. You have.

PAPA BOBBY. Come home, Elizabeth. It doesn't have to be so hard. Come back home.

LIZ. To Holly Grove?

PAPA BOBBY. Yes, sweetheart. We'll do this together.

LIZ. She loves it here. She has Bernie and Enshantay –

PAPA BOBBY. Please Liz. She's…well. She's all we have left of him.

>*(Pause.)*

Y'all come on home.

Scene Sixteen

LIZ. Myron. Thanks for agreeing to see me.

MYRON. Yeah, sure.

LIZ. I am so, so sorry.

MYRON. Okay.

LIZ. I'm sorry.

MYRON. You said that.

LIZ. I'm really, really sorry.

MYRON. Great, I'm glad we have that covered.

LIZ. I'm trying to –

MYRON. What?

LIZ. Apologize to you.

MYRON. And you've done that. Like five times.

LIZ. Myron.

MYRON. What do you want from me? A chapter from some trashy book? You come over, beg me to forgive you, I try to refuse, but I simply cannot resist you. I kiss you, pick you up, throw you on a bed, make love to you and then happily ever after. Wow, I really learned a lot from a real, live romance novelist. You're a liar.

LIZ. I know.

MYRON. I liked you.

LIZ. Why? Why did you like me?

MYRON. I've been doing the New York fucking around thing for a while, Liz. Ever since Stephanie, I've just been doing the New York fucking around thing. Like, none of it mattered. Because I wouldn't let it. Then I met you. And I wanted it to matter. I wanted…it felt real! I thought something real was…I'm so stupid. I thought it was real.

LIZ. It was.

MYRON. After your daughter's birthday party, I was sad and angry. But then I remembered something about the New York fucking around thing: if I get drunk enough and it's late enough and I get enough eye contact across a crowded bar, a bathroom stall with a stranger at four a.m. sure beats the hell out of romance.

LIZ. Wow.

MYRON. I don't have to be nice to someone who's done nothing but lie to me.

LIZ. I am twenty-nine. I have no career. I have a seven-year-old daughter. I am a widow. That's the story. That's my story.

MYRON. I could have handled it. Your story? I could have handled it. I'm actually pretty sensitive. I'm a musician named Myron.

LIZ. No, you couldn't have. I can't even handle / it.

MYRON. Liz?

LIZ. Yes?

MYRON. Please. I don't care. I really don't care.

LIZ. Yes, you do. I know you do.

(She goes to him, he refuses her. Pause.)

I'm leaving. Lily and me. We're moving back to Mississippi. We are going to move in with Lily's grandparents. I am going to live with my daughter, in my dead husband's parents' house. And that's…it. I don't know the ending.

Scene Seventeen

LIZ. Readers have certain expectations: that's the deal. That's why I read romance novels. I am guaranteed a happy ending. A promise is made and kept. I know what is what, the rules are set. Those things, those guidelines, bring me a great deal of comfort. And if the things in this particular book bring you comfort, well. Then. You may continue to read *Whispering Willow: A Story for Children About Dying.*

LILY. You're not mad?

LIZ. I'm not mad. I'm sorry that I took it away from you in the first place. So. How did you get another copy of it?

LILY. …

LIZ. Silly Aunt Bernie?

LILY. I don't know.

LIZ. You can tell me. I won't get mad.

LILY. She gave it to me. For the move.

LIZ. I want you to read anything and everything that Silly tells you to. She knows about some good stuff. Papa Bobby said that they're gonna turn CeeCee's Christmas closet into a costume room for you.

LILY. Really?!

LIZ. Really. And they're gonna fence in the yard, so Spaghetti can cut loose back there and we won't worry about him running into the street.

LILY. Because if he did he would get hit by a car and then he would die.

> *(Beat.)*

LIZ. Yes. That's right. *(Beat.)* Hey, Dill? Can I read some of that with you?

LILY. I thought that you didn't like this book.

LIZ. Well. I've never read it, so I don't really know. You know there's a saying: "Don't judge a book by its cover."

LILY. I know that one. Silly taught me.

LIZ. See? I told you, she knows some good stuff.

LILY. We were walking by one of the Elmos in Times Square and Enshantay said, "Ooh. Those Elmo costumes must be so gross." And then Silly Aunt Bernie said that she used to get freak nasty with a really hot Colombian guy who trains with Twyla Tharp but does the Elmo gig to pay rent because he couldn't get a work visa and that he tickled her juuuust right and that he got his costume professionally dry-cleaned once a week. And then Enshantay said, "I didn't know you used to get freak nasty with an Elmo." And then Silly said that she did and, "Don't judge a book by its cover." So. Yeah. I know that one.

LIZ. Oh. Okay. *(Beat.)* So? May I read this with you?

LILY. Sure, but here's the deal: you have to do voices.

LIZ. Come on, really?

LILY. Please! Silly does the voices so good when we read this!

LIZ. …Okay. I will try to do the voices as good as Silly.

> *(**LIZ** reads.)*

"Whispering Willow: A Story for Children About Dying.
Sam Squirrel and Whispering Willow would play from sun up to sun down. But one morning Sam noticed Whispering Willow's leaves were turning brown. 'What is wrong, Whispering Willow?' Sam Squirrel asked his favorite tree.

'I don't know,' said Whispering Willow. 'Rotting leaves and branches, what could this be?'"

> *(**LILY** is trying not to laugh.)*

See? I told you I'm not good at voices!

LILY. You're so bad at them!

LIZ. Thanks a lot!

LILY. Okay, okay. So just read it as you, as Mama.

> *(A beat. Then **LIZ** reads, as **LILY**'s mama. And, as herself.)*

LIZ. "'I'll go get the Friendly Tree Troll!' Sam exclaimed. 'The very best doctor in town!' But as the Friendly Tree Troll checked her branches, Whispering Willow's leaves fell to the ground."

*(**LIZ** turns the page.)*

Your turn.

LILY. "'What can we do for Whispering Willow?' Sam asked. 'Do her branches just need a good chop?' 'Sam, Whispering Willow is dying,' said the Friendly Tree Troll. 'And we cannot make it stop.'"

*(**LILY** turns the page.)*

Your turn.

LIZ. "'You have to make her better!' Sam yelled, 'Do some Friendly Tree Troll tricks!' 'Sam, there are some things that even us Friendly Tree Trolls cannot fix.' 'What will I do without her?' asked Sam. 'I don't want anything to change.'"

(Beat.)

LILY. Mama.

LIZ. Yes, baby?

LILY. Turn the page.

*(**LIZ** does.)*

End of Play

CPSIA information can be obtained
at www.ICGtesting.com
Printed in the USA
LVHW022019090323
741286LV00002B/247